The Pedlar's Caps

Retellings of this story have appeared in the following collections: *Eurasian Folk and Fairy Tales* (Balapkin); *Carpenter's African Wonder Tales* (Francis Carpenter); *Fairy Tales from the British Isles* (William Ellis); and *Tell Me a Tale: Stories, Songs and Things to Do* (Jean Chapman, published by Hodder & Stoughton, Australia, 1974). A well-loved picture book by Esphyr Slobodkina was published by Harper and Row, New York, 1968.

"Caps for sale," called Dan the pedlar-man. "Warm, woolly nightcaps."

He went uphill and down, all around the town. Fifty woolly nightcaps were piled on top of his own black cap. On his back he carried a big bag of bananas for his lunch.

There was something he didn't see above him.

Swish, swing, jump and spring,
from roof to tree.
Who could it be?

"Caps for sale. Warm, woolly nightcaps."
But no one would buy his caps. No one bought even one single cap.

Uphill and down, right through the town.

Swish, swing, jump and spring,
from tree to tree,
but Dan didn't see.

Monkey Tales

retold by
Laurel Dee Gugler

illustrations by
Vlasta van Kampen

Annick Press • Toronto • New York

Introduction

The three tales in this collection, well-loved for their humour, come from various parts of the world. My delight in these tales motivated me to become part of their ongoing chain of retellings.

Though we don't know exactly what the oldest, oral versions of these stories were like, the published retellings have certain details in common that have persisted over time and may have the originals as their source. Geographical details and other details of my retellings do not attempt to represent a specific culture or region. Inevitably, the author and illustrator bring part of themselves and their cultures to the pool of shared wisdom and joy. The illustrator, for example, chose to portray the primates in a fanciful way. In addition to monkeys, she has depicted orangutans, gorillas, chimpanzees and baboons, though there is no one place on earth where all of them co-exist.

Above all, the retellings in this volume are presented with a deep respect and appreciation for the traditions that contributed to the insight and charm that previous versions convey.

Laurel Gugler
Toronto, 1998

Contents

Feeling dreary, worn and weary, he sat against a tree to rest. There was something he didn't see in that tree. Barely awake, he r e a c h e d and ate... one, two, three, four bananas. He thought that he had more bananas. Where could they be?

"Oh, well." He was too sleepy to care. With yawns and sighs he closed his eyes.

While he slept...
    Swoop, swing, swipe and spring
        down from the tree.
            Who could it be?

When he woke from his nap, he reached for his caps. But, of course, they weren't there—only his own black cap.

He looked this way. No caps.
He looked that way. No caps.
He looked behind him and around—
no caps to be found.

He looked up. What did he see?
Fifty little monkeys sitting in the tree.
Each wore one woolly nightcap.
    Dan the pedlar-man shook a finger.

"Give back my caps!"
Each little monkey shook a finger,
just like Dan.
    "Ch, ch, ch, ch!"

Dan's face turned red. **"Give back
my caps!"** he said.
    He shook a fist.

8

Each little monkey shook a fist,
just like Dan.
    "Ch, ch, ch, ch!"

Dan's mouth turned down.
    He bellowed through his frown.

    "Give back my caps!" He stamped his foot.
    Each little monkey stamped a foot,
just like Dan.
    "Ch, ch, ch, ch!"

Dan's voice became a roar,
    even louder than before.

    "Give back my caps!" He jumped up
and down.
    Each little monkey jumped up and down,
just like Dan.
    "Ch, ch, ch, ch!"

In a rage, he flung his own black cap to the ground...
and each little monkey flung down a cap, **just like Dan.**

"That's better!" said Dan. He gathered all fifty nightcaps and piled them on top of his own black cap.

Dan the pedlar-man went uphill and down, back into the town. "Caps for sale! Warm, woolly nightcaps!"

There was something he didn't see behind him.

Hide, sneak, run and peek
  from bush to tree.
    Who could it be?

Big Monkey's Banana Trouble

Found in Brazilian folklore, this tale shares a theme with an
American Uncle Remus story. It has been retold in the following
collections: *Once upon a Time: Twenty Cheerful Tales to Read and Tell*
(Random House, New York, 1950) and *Fairy Tales
from Brazil* (Elsie Spicer Eells, published by
Dodd, Mead & Co., 1917).

Once upon a time, when the world was new, there was every kind of monkey that you can imagine.

Big ones, small ones,
    short ones, tall ones.
        Frisky, fun-and-tumble ones,
            grouchy, grump-and-grumble ones.

There were **millions** and **billions** of monkeys.

Busy ones, lazy ones,
    drive-you-downright-crazy ones,
        lithe and limber, lanky ones,
            tricky, hanky-panky ones.

But one thing was the same about all of them. They **all** loved bananas!

One of the biggest monkeys was called big monkey. Big monkey knew where the best bananas grew—in little old woman's garden. Aged and bent, each day she went to gather the bananas. But it made her back sore and she bent even more. So she bargained with big monkey.

"If you gather the bananas," she said, "you may have half."

Big monkey agreed. But he kept the large ones and gave her the little ones. Little old woman was oh, *so* angry! She thought of a trick. She made a huge wax statue of a banana pedlar. On his head she placed a basket of big, ripe bananas.

Along came big monkey. Feeling grand, he raised a hand, saluting politely. "Pedlar-man, oh pedlar-man, please give me just **one** banana."

But of course pedlar-man just stood, like any wax-man would. He said not a word. Monkey wondered if he'd heard. He spoke louder, but still politely. **"Pedlar-man, oh pedlar-man, please give me just one banana."**

Pedlar-man said not a word.

Big monkey shook a fist. He called in his loudest voice, not at all politely, **"Pedlar-man, oh pedlar-man, give me just one banana or I'll hit you with my fist."**

Pedlar-man stayed silent.

Big monkey punched pedlar-man.

Whap!

His fist stuck in the wax.

Well! He hooted and howled,
    struggled and yowled,
        but he could **not** get free.

"Let go!" he yelled, **"or I'll hit you with my other fist!"**

Pedlar-man stayed silent. He stood stone-still.

Big monkey punched pedlar-man with his other fist.

Whap!

It stuck, too. What was he to do?

Well! He roared and ranted,
    puffed and panted,
        but he could **not** get free.

"Let go or I'll kick you with my foot!"
Did pedlar-man let go? No! Just stood there, blow
by blow.
    Big monkey kicked pedlar-man.

Thwack!

    His foot stuck, too. What was he to do?

Well! He raged and pranced,
    a one-legged dance,
        but he could **not** get free.

"Let go or I'll kick you with my other foot."
Did pedlar-man let go?
No!

Big monkey kicked pedlar-man with his other foot.

Thwack!

Of course, it stuck, too. What was he to do?

Well! He twisted and jerked,
   went quite berserk,
      but he could not get free.

"Let go or I'll bash you with my head!"
Did pedlar-man let go?
No! No! No!
Big monkey bashed his head into pedlar-man.

Thunk!

Of course, his head stuck, too. There was nothing he could do but howl and yowl like thunder! It made the other monkeys wonder.

What is going on?

They came running from every direction.

Young ones, old ones,
   timid ones and bold ones.
      Hoity-toity, haughty ones,
         mischievous and naughty ones.

Millions and **billions** of monkeys.

Hulky ones, lean ones,
   gentle ones and mean ones.
      Sassy ones, saucy ones,
         burly, booming, bossy ones.

They all wanted to help big monkey.
It was littlest monkey who thought of a plan.
Together they made a mountain of monkeys. All the
monkeys climbed on top of each other. Those with
the loudest voices were on top. All the monkeys
made one big voice. They called to the sun.
   "Please help big monkey!"
The sun heard. Without a word he shone, shone,
shone, hotter than he'd ever shone before.

The pedlar-man began to melt. Big monkey
pulled out his head.

"O-o-oh, my aching neck!" he said.

He pulled out one fist, then the other...
one foot, then the other.

He was free!

Whoop-de-dee!

They danced with monkey glee!

Shouting "thank you" to the sun, they
all joined the fun!

Thousands, millions, billions, trillions!
Even grump-and-grumble ones,
along with fun-and-tumble ones!

And there were plenty of bananas for everyone!
Guess what! There still are!
Enough for **you,** the monkeys and me.

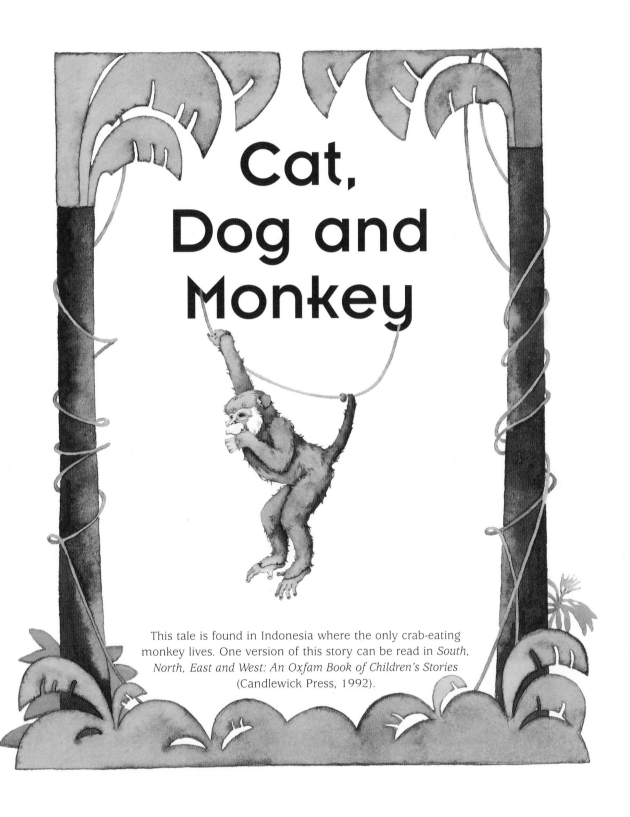

Cat, Dog and Monkey

This tale is found in Indonesia where the only crab-eating monkey lives. One version of this story can be read in *South, North, East and West: An Oxfam Book of Children's Stories* (Candlewick Press, 1992).

Cat and dog quarrelled over some food. Around and around they went, snarling and fighting, clawing and biting, a whirling blur of furious fur.

Joining the flurry, little monkey danced about. Back and forth he pranced. He cheered for cat, then for dog.

Howls and yowls and monkey chatter made an awful rumpus. Cat became tired. Dog became tired. But monkey was spunky as ever.

With a mischievous, sly, wily gleam in his eye, he made a clever suggestion.

"I will divide the food. Cat will get as much as dog. Dog will get as much as cat."

Cat and dog agreed.

Little monkey was ever so clever. He made balance scales with twigs, twine and twisted vines. Cat and dog were impressed.

Monkey divided the food.
    He put a piece on one side.
    He put a piece on the other.
    Up went one side.
    Down went the other.

"Oops!" said little monkey, "one piece is a teeny-tiny bit bigger. But don't worry! I'll just nibble a little from the bigger piece."

Cat and dog were extremely impressed. Monkey was clever as ever. He could solve any problem.

Nibble, nibble, nibble went little monkey.
    He put a piece on one side.
    He put a piece on the other.
    Oh, dear!
    Up went one side.
    Down went the other.

"Oops! I nibbled too much. Now the other side is a teeny-tiny bit bigger! But don't worry! I'll just nibble a little from the other piece."

Cat looked at dog. Dog looked at cat. Cat's belly rumbled. Dog's belly grumbled.

Nibble, nibble, nibble went little monkey.
   He put a piece on one side.
   Not much left for the other.
   Not again!
   Up went one side.
   Down went the other.

"Don't worry!" said little monkey, "I'll fix it."
But cat was no longer impressed. Dog was quite
distressed.

Nibble, nibble, nibble went little monkey.
   A tiny piece on one side.
   A tinier piece on the other.
   Of course **you** know what happened.
   Up went one side.
   Down went the other.

Cat began to yowl. Dog began to growl.
   "Remember," said monkey, "cat must have as
much as dog. Dog must have as much as cat."
   That was quite true. What were they to do?

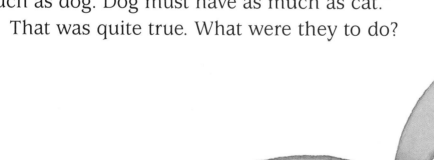

They drooled and dribbled while monkey
nibbled, first on one piece, then the other, **until...**
he popped the last piece in
   with a merry monkey grin.

   "YOWL!" howled cat.
   "HOWL!" yowled dog.
   "BU-R-R-R-RP!" said little monkey, springing
nimbly to a tree. "If you need more help at all,
just call on me."

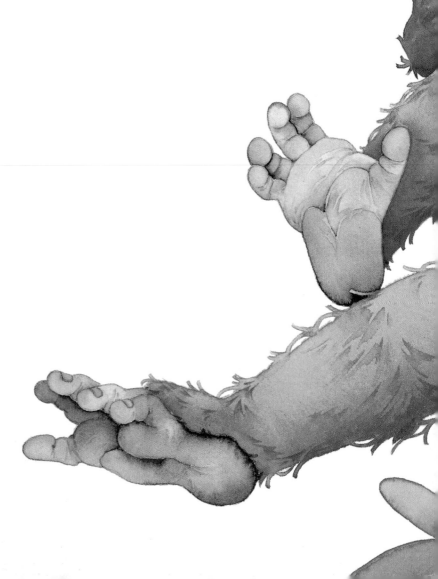

Three tales for three special people –
Kelly, Ellie and Neenee.
L.D.G.

For Frances Hanna, my agent,
who makes it all happen.
V.v.K.

©1998 Laurel Dee Gugler (text)
©1998 Vlasta van Kampen (art)
Designed by Sheryl Shapiro

Annick Press Ltd.

We acknowledge the support of the Canada Council for the Arts for our publishing program. We also thank the Ontario Arts Council.

THE CANADA COUNCIL | LE CONSEIL DES ARTS
FOR THE ARTS | DU CANADA
SINCE 1957 | DEPUIS 1957

Cataloguing in Publication Data
Gugler, Laurel Dee
      Monkey tales

ISBN 1-55037-531-8 (bound) ISBN 1-55037-530-X (pbk.)

1. Monkeys – Indonesia – Folklore. 2. Monkeys – Brazil – Folklore. 3. Monkeys – Europe – Folklore. I. Van Kampen, Vlasta. II. Title.

PS8563.U44M64 1998   j398.24'5298   C98-930214-8
PZ8.1.G83Mo 1998

The art in this book was rendered in watercolours.
The text was typeset in Usherwood.

Distributed in Canada by:
Firefly Books Ltd.
3680 Victoria Park Avenue
Willowdale, ON
M2H 3K1

Published in the U.S.A. by Annick Press (U.S.) Ltd.
Distributed in the U.S.A. by:
Firefly Books (U.S.) Inc.
P.O. Box 1338
Ellicott Station
Buffalo, NY 14205

Printed in Hong Kong.